Guide to
SUPER MEMORY

Dr Shireen Stephen holds a PhD in Health Psychology and an MPhil and MSc in Applied Psychology. She is a counselling psychologist, researcher, writer and editor. Well-known for her episodic memory for remembering dates and connected events, she is also renowned for her auditory memory of remembering clients and their counselling sessions—even years later—without taking down any notes!

Guide to
SUPER MEMORY

Shireen Stephen

RUPA

Published by
Rupa Publications India Pvt. Ltd 2018
7/16, Ansari Road, Daryaganj
New Delhi 110002

Sales centres:
Allahabad Bengaluru Chennai
Hyderabad Jaipur Kathmandu
Kolkata Mumbai

Copyright © Shireen Stephen 2018

The views and opinions expressed in this book are the author's own and the facts are as reported by him which have been verified to the extent possible, and the publishers are not in any way liable for the same.

All rights reserved.
No part of this publication may be reproduced, transmitted, or stored in a retrieval system, in any form or by any means, electronic, mechanical, photocopying, recording or otherwise, without the prior permission of the publisher.

ISBN: 978-93-5304-045-1

Fourth impression 2018

10 9 8 7 6 5 4

The moral right of the author has been asserted.

This book is sold subject to the condition that it shall not, by way of trade or otherwise, be lent, resold, hired out, or otherwise circulated, without the publisher's prior consent, in any form of binding or cover other than that in which it is published.

Chapter 1

Building Blocks of Memory

Memory is the ability to remember something that happened in the past. You experience many things in your daily life through the five senses of touch, taste, smell, sight and sound. Whatever you retain through your five senses is called memory.

You can train yourself to develop a memory that is nothing short of amazing. You can use certain memory techniques to strengthen your memory. By taking the time to learn and practice these techniques, you will find a drastic improvement in your concentration, your thinking will become clearer, your observation skills and self-confidence will improve and you will be able to study effectively by using the least amount of effort. To use memory techniques effectively, you first need to develop your powers of **visualization**, **association**, **imagination** and memory for **locations** since these are the building blocks of memory.

Visualization

Visualization is nothing but creating pictures or images in your mind. It helps you remember people, places and names easily by associating images, colours and impressions with words. For example, if you want to remember that the capital of Bulgaria is Sofia, you can picture a bull (BULgaria) jumping on a sofa (SOFiA). Make your mental pictures as outrageous, crazy and ridiculous as possible. The image can be animated, brightly coloured or completely out of proportion…whatever works for you. Since all this happens inside your head, you don't have to be afraid of anyone laughing at you or judging you.

Visualizations also help bring your study material to life. For example, if you are learning about the composition of the Lok Sabha, have a mental picture in your head of what a session might look like. In your mind, picture the Lok Sabha to be a palace with the Queen (Speaker of the House, currently Sumitra Mahajan) sitting on her high chair and holding court. All 552 (maximum strength of the Lok Sabha) of her subjects are sitting around her in a semi-circle, facing her. Of the 552 members, 530 are wearing red because they represent their States; twenty are wearing blue because they represent the Union Territories and only two members are wearing bright yellow because they represent the Anglo-Indian community. These two members along with the twenty members of the Union Territories are special because they have been nominated directly by the President of India himself while the other representatives of States have been elected by the people. In your mind, you should be able to see a majority of the people in red, a few people in blue and only two spots of bright yellow. Make sure the picture in your head is as funny, bright and loud as possible. Be as outrageous as you can with your creativity. Can you hear each representative shouting something in their own language? What a cacophony it must be!

Visualizations do not need to be exact but even picturing any aspect of the object in question is enough for you to be able to recall it. For example, when asked to visualize a horse, you do not need to have an exact picture of a horse in your mind but even an aspect of a horse, such as its glorious silky mane or its polished, shiny horseshoes, is more than enough to fix the mental picture in your mind. When you are studying long lists of words, you will not have the time to stop and fix a fully accurate mental picture in your mind for every word. What needs to flash in your memory is just a quick image or aspect of the word that you are studying.

Pro Tip: Try to convert your study material into mental images that you can see in your head.

Association

Association simply means connecting two or more things together. Your brain always stores information in the form of connections or associations. Whenever you observe something new, you always connect it with something that you already know. What was subconsciously associated strongly, will be remembered and what was not associated strongly will be forgotten.

It will help you study if you associate any new information with prior information already present in your memory. For example, 'Do Re Me Fa So La Tee Do' (Sa Re Ga Ma Pa Dha Ni Sa) are all associated with the musical notes 'CDEFGABC'. So instead of learning notes as 'C,D,E...' you would learn it as 'Do, Re, Me...,' which is easier to remember than individual letters. However, since the words 'Do, Re, Me...' are also words that make little sense, you can associate them with something that you already know. If you know the song from the movie *The Sound of Music*, it goes:

(Do) doe, a deer, a female deer
(Re!) ray, a drop of golden sun
(Mi!) me, a name I call myself
(Fa!) far, a long, long way to run
(So!) sew, a needle pulling thread
(La!) la, a note to follow so
(Ti!) tea, a drink with jam and bread
That will bring us back to do oh oh oh...

Here, not only are the musical notes of 'CDEFGABC' associated with 'Do Re Me Fa So La Ti Do' respectively, but each association of the words (Do Re Me, etc.) is also connected with something that is familiar to you like female deer, sun, needle, thread, etc.

This helps you put some meaning to the 'nonsense' words by putting in vivid pictures (a drop of golden sun, needle pulling thread, etc.), thus making it easier to remember.

You may tend to think of an object, not in terms of its dictionary definition but rather by the notions that you associate with it. For example, you may not think of rain as condensed moisture from the atmosphere falling in separate drops, but you may have personal associations for it such as snuggling under the blankets on a rainy day, sitting on the balcony and drinking warm milk while it is pouring outside, bike rides in the rain, slushy puddles, getting splashed, shivering in the cold…the list can go on.

> **Pro Tip:** You learn and remember something new by connecting it with something that you already know, but there needs to be a strong association between the two. How clearly you visualize a picture is more important than how long you can visualize it.

Imagination

Imagination is what binds visualizations, associations and locations together. The more absurd the visualization, the stronger is the association and this is achieved by a vivid imagination. Let your imagination run riot. In your head, the laws of physics do not apply. Animals can speak, inanimate objects can juggle or do tricks…anything is possible. The more ridiculous the imagination, the better you will remember what you are studying. Where memory is concerned, there are a few fun principles of imagination to follow to make visualizations and associations stronger.

1. **Exaggeration**: The more imaginative and exaggerated your pictorial associations, the better you will remember them. Exaggeration makes your associations unusual and unique!

2. **Out of proportion**: In all your images, try to distort size and shape. Caricatures and cartoons are perfect for this.
3. **Humour**: Be as funny or as rude and obscene as you want. The funnier you are, the better you remember.
4. **Don't just walk, dance!**: It's easy to say, 'I got bitten by mosquitos'. Instead, you can say: 'I got massacred by a battalion of mosquitos!' When you use more and more movements and action words in the way that you think and express yourself, you will not only remember information better but you will aid your imagination and boost your vocabulary in the process.
5. **'Un' everything**: Unlock, unblock, unleash, unchain, unbar your imagination. Make it as *unusual* as possible.
6. **Sensate**: Use all your senses while visualizing or imagining something. For example. Don't just see that strawberry and vanilla ice cream cone in your mind, feel how cool it is in your hands, the slurping sounds you make as you devour it before the cone becomes mushy! Is the smell of strawberries intoxicating? If you use all your senses to imagine something, it leaves a vivid picture in your mind which you will never forget.
7. **Symbols**: Use symbols whenever possible. This not only shortens the time that you need to encode, but gives you a readymade visual. Symbols also help you memorize abstract concepts.
8. **Practice! Practice! Practice!**: And repeat! Yes, you *can* practice daydreaming. The more you practice, the better you will get at it and the quicker you will be able to form images in your mind.
9. **Order**: It is easier to remember items that are in order rather than jumbled up or unrelated items. Take time to put jumbled items in some sort of order so that you can understand and associate them better.

10. **Enjoy**: Perhaps the most important principle to imagination, and indeed, to anything in life, is to enjoy what you are doing. Make studying a game, give yourself rewards for completing something, challenge yourself to memory games and have fun letting your imagination run riot.

> **Pro Tip**: Let your imagination go wild and unfettered when it comes to associating visuals and locations.

Location

Locations make up the map of memory, providing a natural and efficient way of storing and retrieving memories. This is because the world is three-dimensional and objects can be located—physically or mentally—by where they are placed. Just as it is possible to find a connection between any two sets of information, it is possible for your brain to find an association between any word, object, notion, or thought and a location. Let's take the word 'crayon', for instance. Close your eyes and let your mind wander freely, thinking about this word. Your mind may take you to several places such as your pre-school where you did a lot of colouring, or your grandparents' house where they always kept a box of crayons for you, or a restaurant where you were given two crayons along with the kids' menu, etc. Location, then, is an indispensable building block of memory training because it lends itself well to association.

> **Pro Tip**: Visualizing and associating something new or something to be learnt in the context of their locations will help strengthen the image in your mind.

Chapter 2

Memory Techniques

PART ONE: FUN MEMORY TECHNIQUES

Acronyms

Using acronyms is the easiest method for remembering information, where you take the first letter of each word to be remembered and this, in turn, may (or may not) form another word. Here, the first letter of each word serves as a clue to an item that you need to recall. This is useful when you want to remember words in a specific order, but it is more helpful in just shortening long words to their abbreviations. For example, United Nations Organization is simply shortened to UNO but most of the time, you may just say 'UN'.

How can you apply acronyms while studying? If there is a short enough list of words, you can simply take the first letter of each word and combine them. When you see the initial letters, you should be reminded of the whole word. For example, if you wanted to learn the names of oceans from the largest to the smallest, you can use the acronym '**PAISA**' to represent **P**acific Ocean, **A**tlantic Ocean, **I**ndian Ocean, **S**outhern Ocean and **A**rctic Ocean.

Let's look at a few more examples that may be useful to you while studying.

History and Civics

1. Official languages of the UN: FACERS—**F**rench, **A**rabic, **C**hinese, **E**nglish, **R**ussian, **S**panish.
2. Members of OPEC: QUAKE IS LEAVING—**Q**atar, **U**AE, **A**lgeria, **K**uwait, **E**cuador, **I**ran, **S**audi Arabia, **L**ibya, **E**quatorial Guinea, **A**ngola, **V**enezuela, **I**raq, **N**igeria, **G**abon.
3. Invaders of India in sequence: PDEF—**P**ortugal, **D**utch, **E**nglish, **F**rench.
4. Where was the Harappa civilization located? GPRS—**G**ujarat, **P**unjab, **R**ajasthan, **S**ind.
5. States with Bicameral System: JUMBAKT—**J**ammu & Kashmir, **U**ttar Pradesh, **M**aharashtra, **B**ihar, **A**ndhra Pradesh, **K**arnataka, **T**elangana.

Geography

1. Colours of the rainbow: VIBGYOR—**V**iolet, **I**ndigo, **B**lue, **G**reen, **Y**ellow, **O**range, **R**ed ROY G BIV—**R**ed, **O**range, **Y**ellow, **G**reen, **B**lue, **I**ndigo, **V**iolet.
2. Countries collectively called the Horn of Africa: SEED—**S**omalia, **E**thiopia, **E**ritrea, **D**jibouti.
3. Length of boundaries that India shares with surrounding countries in decreasing order: BaChPaN MBA—**BA**ngladesh, **CH**ina, **PA**kistan, **N**epal, **M**yanmar, **B**hutan, **A**fghanistan.
4. Seven mountain ranges of India: V SHAPES—**V**indhyas, **S**atpuras, **H**imalayas, **A**ravalis, **P**atkai, **E**astern Ghats, **S**ahyadris.
5. ASEAN Countries: BLIMPS C MTV—**B**runei, **L**aos, **I**ndonesia, **M**alaysia, **P**hilippines, **S**ingapore, **C**ambodia, **M**yanmar, **T**hailand, **V**ietnam.

Mathematics

1. The order of operations in Maths (USA): PEMDAS—

Parenthesis, Exponents, Multiplication, Division, Addition, Subtraction.
2. The order of operations in Maths (UK, India and Australia): BODMAS—**B**rackets, **O**rder (**Of**), **D**ivision, **M**ultiplication, **A**ddition, **S**ubtraction.
3. Factoring Binomials: FOIL—**F**irst, **O**uter, **I**nner, **L**ast.
4. How to solve a word problem: SOLVE—**S**tudy the problem, **O**rganize the facts, **L**ine up the plan, **V**erify the plan with computation, **E**xamine the answer.
5. Method for dividing fractions: SMURF—**S**ame, **M**ultiply, **U**pside-down, **R**ename **F**raction.

Biology
1. The phases of mitosis: IPMAT—**I**nterphase, **P**rophase, **M**etaphase, **A**naphase, **T**elophase.
2. ABC of an environment: ABC—**A**biotic (non-living), **B**iotic (living), **C**ultural (man-made).
3. Eight aspects of living organisms: GRRIM END—**G**rowth, **R**espiration, **R**eproduction, **I**rritability, **M**ovement, **E**xcretion, **N**utrition, **D**eath.

English
1. The eight parts of speech in English: PAV PANIC—**P**ronouns, **A**djectives, **V**erbs, **P**repositions, **A**dverbs, **N**ouns, **I**nterjections, **C**onjunctions.
2. The seven coordinating conjunctions in English: FANBOYS—**F**or, **A**nd, **N**or, **B**ut, **O**r, **Y**et, **S**o.

There are a few disadvantages to this system. The first is that if there is more than one word that begins with the same letter, you might get confused about the order of the words. To remedy this, you can take the first two letters of the second word to form an acronym. The second disadvantage is that this method is useful for rote memory, but does not help with comprehension of information. The third disadvantage is that acronyms don't always work for every type of information. Some combination of initials of words may not always lead to another memorable word or short-form. The fourth disadvantage is that there is a danger of forgetting the acronym itself, which will lead to a failure to remember the necessary information. This is why, as with any other memory technique, care should be taken to encode and learn the information at the beginning.

Keep in mind that you need to learn the information in the first place. Acronyms are only memory aids that help you retrieve the information already learnt. For example, you may be able to remember the acronym PAV PANIC, but unless you know what it stands for, remembering the acronym alone is useless.

Acrostics

Acrostics are similar to acronyms, but you take the first letter of each word and form *sentences* with them. For example, the names of the planets in our solar system can be remembered in order by using the acrostic **My Very Elegant Mother Just Served Us Noodles**. When you take the first letter of each word, you get **M**ercury, **V**enus, **E**arth, **M**ars, **J**upiter, **S**aturn, **U**ranus and **N**eptune. This method is handy in remembering passwords, formulae and long lists of words that need to be memorized in order. If your words don't form easy to remember acronyms, you can just make up ridiculous sentences to remember them.

Biology

1. In Taxonomy, you can remember the order of rankings by remembering this acrostic:
   Keep **P**ots **C**lean **O**therwise **F**amilies **G**et **S**ick
   Kingdom, **P**hylum, **C**lass, **O**rder, **F**amily, **G**enus, **S**pecies

2. Phases of mitosis:
   I **P**icked **M**any **A**pples **T**oday/ **I** **P**ropose **M**en **A**re **T**oads
   Interphase, **P**rophase, **M**etaphase, **A**naphase, **T**elophase
3. The levels of organization from smallest to biggest in Ecology:
   Idiot, **P**lease **C**arry **E**veryone's **Bi**ology **B**ooks
   Individual, **P**opulation, **C**ommunity, **E**cosystem, **Bi**ome, **B**iosphere
4. The eight facial bones:
   Varun **C**an **M**ake **M**y **P**et **Z**ebra **L**augh
   Vomer, **C**onchae, **N**asal, **M**axilla, **M**andible, **P**alatine, **Z**ygomatic, **L**acrimal
5. The eight wrist bones:
   She **L**ooks **T**oo **P**retty, **T**ry **T**o **C**atch **H**er
   Scaphoid, **L**unate, **T**riquetrum, **P**isiform, **T**rapezium, **T**rapezoid, **C**apitate, **H**amate.

Mathematics

1. Trigonometric Ratios:
   Sin = **P**erpendicular/**H**ypotenuse   **S**ome **P**eople **H**ave
   Cos = **B**ase/**H**ypotenuse   **C**urly **B**lack **H**air
   Tan = **P**erpendicular/**B**ase   **T**urning **P**ermanently **B**rown
2. Metric System:
   King **H**enry **D**ied **B**y **D**rinking **C**hocolate **M**ilk
   Kilo, **H**ecto, **D**eca, **B**ase, **D**eci, **C**enti, **M**illi
3. Circumference of a circle:
   Cherry **P**ies, **D**elicious!
   C = **pi** x **d** where C is the circumference and d is the diameter.
4. Area of a circle:
   Apple **P**ies a**R**e **Square**
   A = **pi** x **r**^{2} where A is area and r is radius
5. Roman numerals:
   I **V**alue **X**ylophones **L**ike **C**ows **D**ig **M**ilk

I = 1, V = 5, X = 10, L = 50, C = 100, D = 500, M = 1000

Chemistry

1. First 20 elements in the periodic table:—
   Happy Henry Lives Beside Boron Cottage, Near Our Friend Nelly Nancy MgAllen. Silly Patrick Stays Close. Arthur Kisses Carrie.
   H—Hydrogen, He—Helium, Li—Lithium, Be—Beryllium, B—Boron, C—Carbon, N—Nitrogen, O—Oxygen, F—Fluorine, Ne—Neon, Na—Sodium, Mg—Magnesium, Al—Aluminium, Si—Silicon, P—Phosphorus, S—Sulphur, Cl—Chlorine, Ar—Argon, K—Potassium, Ca—Calcium.
2. Electrochemical Cell: Oxidation Vs Reduction
   AN OIL RIG CAT
   At the ANode, Oxidation Involves Loss of electrons. Reduction Involves Gaining electrons at the CAThode.
3. Diatomic molecules:
   I Have No Bright Or Clever Friends.
   Iodine, Hydrogen, Nitrogen, Bromine, Oxygen, Chlorine, Fluorine.
4. Carboxylic Acids (first six):
   Frogs Are Polite, Being Very Courteous.
   Formic, Acetic, Propionic, Butyric, Valeric, Caproic.
5. Dicarboxylic Acids (first nine):
   Oh My! Such Great Apple Pie! Sweet As Sugar!
   Oxalic, Malonic, Succinic, Glutaric, Adipic, Pimelic, Suberic, Azelaic, Sebacic.

Physics

1. Electromagnetic Spectrum: In order of increasing wavelength of electromagnetic waves.
   Good Xylophones Use Very Interesting Musical Rhythms.
   Gamma Rays, X-rays, Ultraviolet, Visible light, Infrared,

Microwaves, Radio Waves.
2. Colour codes used in electronics, in numerical order:
   Bill **Brown R**ealized **O**nly **Y**esterday, **G**ood **B**oys **V**alue **G**ood **W**ork.
   Black (0), **Brown** (1), **R**ed (2), **O**range (3), **Y**ellow (4), **G**reen (5), **B**lue (6), **V**iolet (7), **G**rey (8), **W**hite (9).

Geography

1. Rivers in North West India:
   I Just **Ch**ecked **B**eautiful **R**iver **S**urveys.
   Indus, **J**helum, **Ch**enab, **B**eas, **R**avi, **S**atluj.
2. Levels of atmosphere:
   Typical, **S**uper **M**ario's **T**ime **E**xpired.
   Troposphere, **S**tratosphere, **M**esosphere, **T**hermosphere, **E**xosphere.
3. Water Cycle:
   Every **C**ook **P**eels **R**ed **G**rapes.
   Evaporation, **C**ondensation, **P**recipitation, **R**unoff, **G**roundwater.

French

1. Days of the week in French:
   Large **M**ean **M**onkeys **J**umped **V**ery **S**lowly **D**own.
   Lundi, **M**ardi, **M**ercredi, **J**eudi, **V**endredi, **S**amedi, **D**imanche.

While studying, try and make your own acrostics—you will remember them better. As with acronyms, acrostics are simply a memory aid but do not help with understanding the information. The disadvantage is that you may forget the phrase or sentence or may substitute words with similar words and therefore, get the initials wrong. Knowing the acrostic is not enough—you need to learn the information first. For example, just remembering 'Large mean monkeys jumped very slowly down' may only lead you to the initials of LMMJVSD, but unless you know what they stand for, using acrostics would be pointless.

Rhymes and Music

You can put your study material into a familiar song so that you can remember it just by singing it. This works with any kind of information, including formulae and definitions. For example, facts about an isosceles triangle can be learnt by singing the following to the tune of 'Oh Christmas Tree'.

> *Oh, isosceles, oh, isosceles,*
> *Two angles have equal degrees.*
> *Oh, isosceles, oh, isosceles*
> *You look just like a Christmas tree.*

You can make up a rhyme about anything that you are studying, which makes your study material easier to remember. Some examples are given below.

1. In the year 1947, India reached Independence heaven!
2. Converting a pint to a pound: *A pint is a pound the whole world around!*
3. Area and circumference of a circle:
   > *Tweedle-dum and Tweedle-dee,*
   > *Around the circle is pi times d,*
   > *But if the area is declared,*
   > *Think of the formula pi 'r' squared.*

   'Around the circle' is the circumference.
   Circumference = pi x d (diameter).
   Area = pi x r (radius) squared.

4. In chemistry, always remember to add acid to water and **not** the other way around!
   Always do things as you oughta

Add the acid to the water.
If you think your life's too placid,
Add the water to the acid.

5. When multiplying with negative numbers, is the answer positive or negative? Here's a way to remember. This is not a rhyme, but it makes it easier to understand the outcome of multiplying with negative numbers. (In this technique, 'good' is positive and 'bad' is negative.)

A good thing happening to a good person is good. (Positive x positive = positive.)
A good thing happening to a bad person is bad. (Positive x negative = negative.)
A bad thing happening to a good person is bad. (Negative x positive = negative.)
A bad thing happening to a bad person is good. (Negative x negative = positive.)

Number Phrase Technique

This technique helps you remember long numbers just by using the same number of letters in words as the number. For example, 'my' has two letters, so denotes the number 2. 'Terrible' has eight letters and so denotes the number 8.

Do you want to learn the value of pi up to the fifteenth digit? Here it is! All you need to do is remember this phrase and count the number of letters in each word and you have your answer!

Value of pi: 3.1415265358979

How I want a drink, alcoholic of course, after the
  3 1 4   1 5   9   2   6   5   3
heavy lectures involving quantum mechanics.
  5   8   9   7   9

                        or
May I have a large container of coffee?
3   1   4   1   5   9   2   6
                        or
How I wish I could calculate pi
3   1   4   1   5   9   2

a) Value of 'e' (exponential function) up to the eighth digit: 2.7182818

    To express 'e', remember to memorize a sentence
    2   7   1   8   2   8   1   8
                  or
    By omnibus I travelled to Brooklyn
    2   7   1   9   2   8

b) Speed of light in metres per second:—2.99792458
    We guarantee certainly, clearly referring to this light mnemonic
    2   9   9   7   9   2   4   5   8

With this technique, be careful to remember the phrase or sentence word for word. If you substitute a word or add or subtract a word, the corresponding number will be wrong. For example, instead of 'large container', if you say 'big container', you will get the value of pi wrong because you will be writing down a 3 (b-i-g) instead of a 5 (l-a-r-g-e).

Mental Snapshot Technique

This technique helps you take a mental photograph or a snapshot of your surroundings and saves the image in your mind. By engaging your full concentration in the present moment, this technique encourages the formation of clearer, stronger memories of important scenes. This method uses three basic and simple memory skills: looking, snapping and then connecting.

    How do you 'snap' a picture? This is nothing but making sure that the picture is 'burnt' into your mind. You can do this by blinking your eyes and imagining that they are the shutter of a camera. If you are on holiday and you would like to remember the scenery, you first look closely and pay attention to the scene, create a mental snapshot of that scene and then connect it with the town or city that you are in. For example, you're on a beach in Goa, watching an amazing sunset. First, pay attention to the details around you. There may be children playing in the sand nearby, the sky may be multi-coloured, the ocean may be reflecting the sunlight and changing colour accordingly. Fix your gaze on the image that you would like to 'burn' into your memory and then capture it in your mind. This means that when you close your eyes, you should be able to see this image clearly in your mind. Now connect this image to the place. For example, Goa, 2018. In the future, whenever you think of this vacation or of a sunset or Goa, you will always have this image in your mind.

If you are studying for your algebra exam and you would like to remember the quadratic equation, first look at it. Observe the equation and all its components. Here, x is the unknown while a, b and c are constants.

$$x = \frac{-b \pm \sqrt{b^2 - 4ac}}{2a}$$

Once you have observed the equation, the next step is to snap your picture. Make sure that the image of the equation is 'burnt' into your mind so that you can still see it when you close your eyes. The third step is to make connections so that if someone asks you what the quadratic equation is, you should be able to immediately recall this image.

The Mental Snapshot Technique is generally used to remember names and faces. But you can also use it to picture formulae and diagrams from your textbooks.

Chapter 3

Memory Techniques

PART TWO: LINKING

Learning Through Linking

The link system of memory is one of the easiest techniques to master. It makes use of all the building blocks of memory but relies heavily on association and visualization. This system can be used to memorize anything in sequence such as speeches, lists, daily schedules, errands, long numbers, formulae, recipes, history timelines, etc. Simply put, it functions by associating items with each other by using your imagination in the most ridiculous, funny, or bizarre way. There are two link methods—the Pure Link Method and the Story Link Method.

Pure Link Method

Do you think you can remember a list of twenty unrelated words in the correct order? Of course you can! Let's see how to go about it. Here are the words:

> *telephone, shadow, paper, fish, violin, bed, rose, book, chicken, sun, cheese,*
> *umbrella, window, mall, ice cream, carpet, computer, mangoes, shampoo, cat*

Okay, now let's see how to link these words so that they can be remembered in order. Since your brain tends to remember and associate things in pairs, you need to work with two words at a time. Here, two words form one link. First take words 1 and 2, then 2 and 3, then 3 and 4, and so on.

The first pair to remember is telephone and shadow. Now, the most practical picture that would come to mind may be a shadow holding a telephone to its ear, but your aim is to make the images in your mind as bright, loud and absurd as possible so that you can remember the associations easily. Can you picture a pink shadow juggling five telephones in its hands? Or imagine rubbing a telephone and a shadow pops out of it like a genie from a lamp! See that image clearly in your mind.

Now move on to words 2 and 3—shadow and paper. When you move on to the next set of words, the previous word is ignored for the time being. So putting the word telephone aside, focus on shadow and paper. Imagine a shadow made of paper, being blown about by the wind while on his evening walk. Fix that image in your mind.

Words 3 and 4—paper and fish. Keep the word shadow aside for now and focus on paper and fish. Can you picture a fish somersaulting over a sea of paper? Every time the fish 'splashes' down, a sheaf of papers flies all over the place like a fountain.

Fish and violin—you're playing a violin at a big concert but instead of a bowstring, you are using a fish!

Violin and bed—a bed made of violins that plays music to you as you fall asleep. You don't even need an alarm clock in the morning since you have your violin bed to wake you up!

Bed and rose—you wake up in bed to find hundreds of rose petals cascading around you gently. All of a sudden, that gentle shower of petals becomes heavy, spikey roses, forcing you to take cover under your bed!

Rose and book—a book's pages made of rose petals and bookmarked with paper.

Book and chicken—you enter class, and, sitting in your

teacher's chair, is a gigantic chicken wearing reading glasses, squinting at a book. It looks at you over its glasses. 'Surprise!' it squawks in a dry voice.

Chicken and sun—as the sun rises, you open your windows to let the sunshine in, but instead a brood of chickens bursts in and starts watching TV.

Can you work out the rest of the words?

Sun and cheese _____
Cheese and umbrella _____
Umbrella and window _____
Window and mall _____
Mall and ice cream _____
Ice cream and carpet _____
Carpet and computer _____
Computer and mangoes _____
Mangoes and shampoo _____
Shampoo and cat _____

Now close your eyes and see the associations clearly in your mind starting from telephone and ending with cat. Were you able to remember all twenty words?

Story Link Method

Another method for linking unrelated words is to make up a story using all the words in the same sequence. We'll use the same words as above.

> Once upon a time, in the land of **telephone**, there lived a **shadow** who liked to juggle. He could juggle anything from **papers** to **fish** to **violins**! He was so good at juggling that he could do it even lying down on his **bed** or upside down! Other shadows came from all over the world to watch his performances. They would often throw **roses** on stage to show their appreciation or **books** or **chickens**

at him if they did not like his act. Since shadows often disappear when the **sun** is out, he carried a **cheese umbrella** and avoided all **windows**. At the **mall**, the shadow gulped down an **ice cream** which made him feel woozy and he fainted right there on the **carpet**! They used the mall **computer** to order **mango** flavoured **shampoo** to revive him. He then went home to juggle his shadow **cat**!

Pro Tips
- Make the images in your mind as bright, loud and as absurd as possible.
- As you make up the story, *visualize* it happening. This is what drills it into your long-term memory. If you can see it in your mind's eye like a movie, you'll automatically remember it afterwards.
- When moving from the first set of linked words, set the first word aside while moving on to the next pair. For example, after pairing 1 and 2, set 1 aside while you move on to 2 and 3. Remember that you are always associating the previous object to the present object.
- Take only about a split second per association. You may take longer at first but as you practice associations, you will be able to conjure up visual images in an instant! Although the above explanations are long, the actual exercise will take you only two or three minutes.
- Do not try to visualize the words themselves, but focus on the pictures that they bring to your mind.
- In case you forget a word, try and remember the next word and then work your way backwards.

While the pure link method is more or less reliable, the story link method is not so reliable as you may deviate from the original plot of the story and forget the sequence or even the words that you need to remember! This is why it is important to *see* the associations clearly in your mind. If you are using the story link method, try to see the story like a movie in your head.

Since you may not remember all the words in sequence in the story link method, use it for lists that do not require an order or a sequence, such as a shopping list or your chores for the day. Use the pure link method to remember the sequence of events in history or a speech or a telephone number.

Chapter 4

Memory Techniques

PART THREE: PEGGING

Imagine your cupboard full of hangers and clothes hanging on each hanger. While the hangers never change, the clothes that you hang on them will keep changing. This is the same principle that is used in Pegging. While your memory pegs never change, what you associate with them will keep changing. From now on, you will be able to 'hang' anything you wish to remember involving numbers or alphabets in any way, on these pegs!

Memory pegs are things that you know well, in a set order. There are two basic pegs—pegs for numbers and pegs for alphabets. To memorize a list, you associate the first item to the first peg, the second item to the second peg and so on. In case you forget an item, you can leave that peg empty and move on. You will be able to remember the next peg since remembering it does not depend on remembering the previous peg like the Link System.

On a daily basis, you need to be able to remember your credit card number, Aadhaar card number, telephone numbers, ATM PIN numbers, passwords, addresses, student identification number, etc. Since numbers are abstract concepts, they have very little meaning. The Number Shape System, the Number Rhyme System and the Major System of Number Pegging will help you ascribe some meaning to these numbers by associating them with specific words or pictures, which you can then visualize better by using your imagination. The Alphabet Peg System can help you memorize long lists of words, schedules, poems, speeches etc. in their correct order.

As with everything related to studying, the key is to keep revising the lists in the Number Peg System and the Alphabet Peg System until the numbers and alphabets along with their respective associated images are second nature to you.

THE NUMBER PEG SYSTEM

The Number Peg System consists of three systems namely—the Number Shape System, the Number Rhyme System and the Major System. These systems are important and are used to memorize history dates, anniversaries and long numbers such as telephone numbers, Aadhaar card numbers, passport numbers, credit card numbers, etc.

The Number Shape System

This system is easy and uses only numbers from 0 to 10. This memory technique works by associating specific numbers to an image that has the same shape or a similar shape to its corresponding number. For example, the open sails of a sailboat resemble the number 4 while the curved trunk of an elephant resembles the number 6. The peg pictures below are the standard pictures that memory geniuses use to visualize numbers. You can either use these images or pick your own for each number. You may write your own peg words or draw your own peg shapes in the last column. Make them as colourful as possible.

Number	Pegs	Alternate Pegs	Your Own Pegs
0–Donut		football, hula hoop, key ring	

1–Candle		stick, paintbrush, spear	
2–Duck		swan, clothes hanger	
3–Heart		butterfly's wings	
4–Sailboat		playground slide	
5–Seahorse		S hook, snake shaped like 5	
6–Elephant trunk		golf club, hockey stick	

26 • *Guide to Super Memory*

7–Candy cane		axe, boomerang	
8–Snowman		hourglass	
9–Tennis racket		round balloon on a string	
10–Girl + Hula hoop		stick + hoop, bat + ball	

Let's try this method with a list of ten words that need to be remembered. Keep in mind that you need to use the shapes associated with the numbers, not the numbers themselves.

office, joy, train, shop, flowers, ocean, cricket, study, car, tree

List these words in the order that you would like to remember them, next to each peg.

1. Candle — Office
2. Duck — Joy
3. Heart — Train
4. Sailboat — Shop
5. Seahorse — Flowers
6. Elephant's trunk — Ocean
7. Candy cane — Cricket

Memory Techniques • 27

    8. Snowman   Study
    9. Tennis racket   Car
   10. Girl hula hooping   Tree

Once this is done, go back to the Link System and link each word to their associated peg.

1. Candle and office: A melting office building made entirely of lit candles.
2. Duck and joy: A mother duck joyfully frolicking with her ducklings.
3. Heart and train: I love trains! Or heart-shaped train tracks.
4. Sailboat and shop: A sailboat crashing into a shop.
5. Seahorse and flowers: A seahorse wearing a tiara of flowers on its head.
6. Elephant's trunk and ocean: A thirsty elephant drinking up all the water in the ocean through its trunk!
7. Candy cane and cricket: Playing cricket using a candy cane instead of a bat.
8. Snowman and study: A snowman studying how to keep cool in the summer.
9. Tennis racket and car: A car in the rain with its tennis-racket-windscreen wipers on.
10. Girl hula hooping and tree: A tree hula hooping while balancing a girl on its highest branch.

Now, just by remembering the associations between the words and their pegs, can you remember them in their correct order?

    Pro Tip: Some words such as joy, love, prayer, peace, etc. are abstract words with no concrete images. You will need to conjure up a concrete image for these words or use them as they are in your associations, for example, 'Joyfully frolicking'.

The Number Rhyme System

The Number Rhyme System is very similar to this nursery rhyme. In this method, numbers are represented by images of things that rhyme with each number. The rhyming words are then used as peg words to remember short numbers or a smaller list of items such as to-do lists, recipes, shopping lists, ATM PINs, phone numbers, flight numbers, hotel room numbers, appointment times, birthdays, history timelines, etc. This method is usually used for numbers 0 to 10, but you can come up with your own rhyming words for number 11 and above.

Given below are a list of numbers with their associated pegs or rhyming words and images. While this is a generic list, please feel free to use your own rhyming words that you are more comfortable with.

Number	Pegs	Peg Image	Alternate Pegs	Your Own Pegs
0	Hero		Bureau	
1	Bun		Sun, Nun	
2	Shoe		Zoo, Glue	
3	Tree		Bee, Knee	

Number	Pegs	Peg Image	Alternate Pegs	Your Own Pegs
4	Door		Floor, Store	
5	Hive		Hard drive	
6	Sticks		Bricks, Ticks	
7	Heaven		Raven, Oven	
8	Gate		Bait, Plate	
9	Wine		Twine, Valentine	
10	Hen		Pen, Den	

Take as much time as you need to memorize the peg words and picture a clear image of the peg words in your mind. Now let's see how you can use this method to remember your busy schedule.

9 a.m.—Fill petrol in car.
10 a.m.—Team meeting.
11 a.m.—Breakfast meeting with a client.
12 p.m.—Return book to the library.
12.30 p.m.—Pickup clothes from laundromat.
2 p.m.—Pick up son from school.
4 p.m.—Print flight tickets.
5 p.m.—Stop at ATM on the way to the airport.
8 p.m.—Flight to Delhi.

In this exercise, since time is in numbers, you can directly associate the time to the particular task. Since you also have two additional numbers of 11 o'clock and 12 o'clock, take a minute to associate appropriate rhyming words. You can denote '12.30' by adding a 'half' to whatever you rhyme number 12 with. For the purpose of this exercise, you can rhyme 11 to lemon and 12 to shelf. You can picture 12.30 to be one shelf plus another half shelf or another shelf broken in half. Now, you can start the associations with the peg words.

9 a.m.—Fill petrol in car—imagine filling up your car with **wine** instead of petrol.
10 a.m.—Team meeting—a big fat **hen** squawks out the presentation at the team meeting.
11 a.m.—Breakfast meeting with client—imagine you and your client eating breakfast out of a gigantic **lemon**!
12 p.m.—Return book to library—picture the library to be an enormous **shelf** that you need to heave the book into.
12.30 p.m.—Pick up clothes from laundromat—clothes are overflowing from one **shelf** into **half** of the next!

Can you work out the remaining associations?

2 p.m.—Pick up son from school_____
4 p.m.—Print flight tickets_____

5 p.m.—Stop at ATM_____
8 p.m.—Flight to Delhi_____

Were you able to visualize the pictures clearly? If you were not able to remember, it could be because:
- You made associations that you did not like.
- The associations were too close or similar to each other.
- There was not enough exaggeration.
- The images that you imagined were not strong enough.
- There was not enough movement.
- The links were too weak or the associations between numbers and their pegs were too weak.
- Perhaps there was not enough humour involved.

The Major System

The Major System is used to convert numbers to letters which are then converted to memorable words. This system helps you remember longer numbers such as your passport number, Aadhaar card number, credit card number, multiple phone numbers, formulae, etc. easily.

In this method, you must first learn a simple phonetic alphabet. Phonetic alphabets are nothing but the sounds that a particular letter makes. For example, instead of saying 't' as in 'tea,' you say 'tuh'; and instead of saying 'n' as in 'en,' you say 'nuh'. You need to learn only ten basic sounds which can be memorized within ten minutes! Just follow the retrieval cues for each sound and you will never forget it!

The basic concept of the system is that it makes use of different consonants or consonant sounds for each number from 0 to 9 using a special code. Here is the list from 0 to 9:

0—s, z, soft c (c with the 'suh' sound as in 'cent')
1—t, d, th
2—n

3—m
4—r
5—l
6—j, sh, ch, soft g (g with the 'juh' sound as in 'general')
7—k, hard c (cuh sound), hard g (guh sound), qu (q has a kuh sound)
8—f, v
9—b, p

Retrieval Cues 1

0—The letter 's' or 'z' is the first sound of the word 'zero' while 'o' is the last letter. The letter 'c' with the 'suh' sound is also used for the number 0.
1—The letters 't' and 'd' have one downward stroke.
2—The letter 'n' has two downward strokes.
3—The letter 'm' has three downward strokes.
4—'Four' in many languages ends with an 'r'. For example, chaar in Hindi, katër in Albanian, vier in Dutch and German, pedwar in Welsh and quarter in Latin.
5—If you hold five fingers up on your left hand, your index finger and thumb form the letter 'L' like . The Roman numeral for number 50 is also L.
6—The mirror image of '6' looks like 'j' and 'g' (pronounced as 'juh').
7—Two number 7s can be used to form the letter 'K'—one 7 right side up and the other, upside down like so K. 'Guh' sounds like 'kuh' and so the letters g, c and q are also used for the number 7.
8— in cursive writing, 'f' has two loops just like the number 8. sounds like 'fuh'.
9—'p' and 'b' are the mirror images of number 9.

Memory Techniques • 33

Retrieval Cue 2

The following phrase will help you remember the letters in the correct sequence:
$$1\ 2\ 3\ 4\ 5\ 6\ 7\ 8\ 90$$
$$\text{TeN MoRe LoGiC FiBS}$$

Retrieval Cue 3

Make up a ridiculous rhyme with the numbers and their associated letters and sounds:

One **T**ied his **T**iny **T**oes,
Two **N**early **N**ever **Kn**ows.
Three **M**elted **M**oney **M**ore,
Four **R**arely **R**eally **R**oared!
Five **L**oved a **L**ittle **L**amp,
Six Was **J**ealous of His **J**am.
Seven **K**issed a **K**angaroo
Eight **F**lipped His **F**lutey **F**oo.
Nine **B**ooped a **B**uzzing **B**ee
Zero **Z**igzagged Through the **S**ea.

Keep repeating the numbers and associated sounds till they are second nature to you, practicing everywhere you go. If you see a licence plate number '4737', you should be able to immediately think 'rkmk' or when you see an address '45/13', you should be able to convert it into 'rl/tm' immediately. Also, whenever you see random words in your everyday life, such as store names and words on billboards etc. you should be able to convert them into numbers. For example, 'Motor Minds' can easily be converted to 314 3210 and Lion Bubble Gum to 52 995 73.

Pro Tips:
- These sounds will **always** be associated with the same numbers.
- **Sounds** of letters are more important than the letters themselves.
- Since only sounds are taken into consideration, silent letters in words are ignored. For example, the 'k' in 'knee, knock and knife' and the 'p' in 'psalm' are ignored.
- Vowels are never used for pegs. Consonants that sound like vowels such as w, h and y are also not used as pegs. For example, 'Buy Now' will be converted to '9 2'!
- Letters that sound alike are used to represent one number. For example, 'v' and 'f' make 'vuh' and 'fuh' sounds that sound alike and represent the number 8.
- Some letters represent different numbers based on their sounds. For example, 'c' as in 'cyst' represents the number 0 while 'c' as in 'carry' represents the number 7. In the same way, 'g' as in 'goat' represents the number 7 while 'g' as in 'gender' represents the number 6.
- Double consonants such as 'tt' 'mm' 'll' are counted as a single consonant since they have the same sound as a single consonant. Therefore, the word 'commitment' is phonetically read as 'comitment' and 'professor' is phonetically read as 'profeser'.
- Double letters pronounced differently in the same word represent two different numbers. For example, 'accept' is pronounced as 'aksept' and 'k' and 's' represent 7 and 0 respectively.
- When there is a word that has a combination of two different letters having the same sound, it is denoted only by one number. For example, the word 'pick' has a 'c' and 'k' which have the 'cuh' sound and, therefore, are denoted with the single number 7 not 77. However, if

the same sound has two syllables in the same word, they are represented twice by the same number. For example, pea**c**o**ck** is represented as 977. Remember, you only go by the sound of the word not the number of letters it has.
- Words that are made by converting the numbers need not be real words. Made-up words can be used as long as you can remember them. For example, you may not be able to think of a word for the numbers 155, but you can use a made-up word—Taloola—to remember it.
- You can use words from different languages not just English, as long as the sounds are the same for each number. For example, you can convert the number 64 to **ch**a**ar** instead of **ch**air if you are more comfortable with Hindi.
- In case you cannot make a phrase or sentence with long numbers, use the Link System to visualize linking the words together.

Advancing the Major System of Pegging

So far, we have talked about pegging sounds for numbers from 0 to 9. Now, we will see how to make up a word for any number, no matter how many digits it contains. Using the same phonetic sounds that were used for numbers 0 to 9, you can think of peg words that use the same sounds for each number and then peg those to their respective numbers. This way they will never change. In future, whenever you hear that particular number, you should be able to remember its corresponding peg word.

Let's begin with the numbers that you already know. You know that the sounds associated with '0' are 's' and 'z' so, an appropriate peg word for '0' that has only these sounds may be 'his' or 'hiss'. This word will now, always be associated with the number '0.' You can pick what you are comfortable with.

In the same way, the number 1 is represented by the sounds that 't' and 'd' make. You can add in additional sounds of 'th' and 'dh' since they sound similar. Now, think of a word that has just one 't, d, th or dh' sound. For now, you can use the word 'tie.' If you translate the word 'tie' into numbers, it is denoted by the number 1. So from now on, the word 'tie' will always be used to denote the number 1.

Moving on to two-digit numbers, the number 11 has two ones and therefore, the word that you use needs to have two sounds of 't' or 'd' or 'th'. How about 'tot?' You can also use the following words—tit, tat, tut, that, thud, dad, did, dud, etc.

The number 12 has a 1 and 2 and therefore, you can use the associated sounds for the numbers 1 and 2 which are 't, d, th, dh and n'. Therefore, you can represent the number 12 by words such as den, ten, then, tin, din, thin, etc.

Let's work out the numbers from 0 to 100. You are welcome to write down your own words. If you are comfortable with a different language, you are free to use words of that language—just make sure to use the correct sounds of 's, t, n, m, r, l, j, k, f' and 'b' (and similar sounds of 'd, c', etc.) to denote the numbers 0, 1, 2, 3, 4, 5, 6, 7, 8 and 9 respectively.

Number	Peg Word	Your own word
0	Hiss	
1	Tie	
2	Noah	
3	Ma	
4	Row	
5	Law	
6	Jaw	
7	Cow	
8	Foe	
9	Bee	
10	Toes	

Memory Techniques

Number	Peg Word	Your own word
11	Tot	
12	Den	
13	Tin	
14	Tire	
15	Toll (Booth)	
16	Taj (Mahal)	
17	Tick	
18	Dove	
19	Tub	
20	Nose	
21	Net	
22	Nun	
23	Numb (num)	
24	Henry	
25	Nail	
26	Nudge	
27	Neck	
28	Knife	
29	Nib	
30	Moose	
31	Mat	
32	Man	
33	Mom	
34	More	
35	Mule	
36	Match	
37	Mickey	
38	Movie	
39	Map	

Number	Peg Word	Your own word
40	Rice	
41	Rod	
42	Run	
43	Rain	
44	Roar	
45	Rail	
46	Raja	
47	Rock	
48	Roof	
49	Robe	
50	Lace	
51	Loot	
52	Loony	
53	Lamb (lam)	
54	Leer	
55	Lolly	
56	Leash	
57	Lake	
58	Laugh (laf)	
59	Lap	
60	Juice	
61	Jut	
62	Chain	
63	Chime	
64	Chore	
65	Jail	
66	Judge (juj)	
67	Joke	
68	Chef	

Number	Peg Word	Your own word
69	Job	
70	Case	
71	Cut	
72	Acorn	
73	Come	
74	Car	
75	Coal	
76	Cage	
77	Cake	
78	Café	
79	Cup	
80	Fuss	
81	Feet	
82	Fan	
83	Fame	
84	Fire	
85	Fall	
86	Fudge (fuj)	
87	Fish	
88	Five	
89	Fab	
90	Bus	
91	Bat	
92	Bun	
93	Bomb (bom)	
94	Bar	
95	Ball	
96	Barge (baj)	
97	Buck	

Number	Peg Word	Your own word
98	Barf (baf)	
99	Puff	
100	Daisies	

Yes, this long list does look a little daunting but since you now have the basic concept, even if you were to forget the peg word, you can just put the sounds of numbers together and remember it. For example, if you forget the peg word for the number 98, you know that 9 has the sound 'b' and 8 has the sound 'f' so if you put the two sounds together (bf), you should be able to remember the word 'barf'.

This is an important memory system which can be used to memorize long numbers in mathematics, the periodic table, addresses, telephone numbers, Aadhaar card numbers and just about any number that you require on a day-to-day basis so it helps to be thorough with this system. Practice by converting any number that you see into words and words into numbers.

THE ALPHABET PEG SYSTEM

The Alphabet Peg System can be used to remember random alphabets such as a PNR numbers, alphanumeric passwords, formulae and long lists of words. You can use familiar peg words to remember lists, long speeches, etc. in the correct order.

Familiar Peg Words

Remember how you learnt the alphabet in kindergarten? A for apple, B for ball, C for cat, etc. Well, this is exactly how the alphabet peg system works. Here, instead of numbers, you use letters A—Z and use their associated words to remember lists that have more than ten items. Here's a list of familiar associated words that you may have grown up with. You can either use these words or use words that you are more comfortable with.

Alphabet	Peg Word	Your Own Word
A	Apple	
B	Ball	
C	Cat	
D	Dog	
E	Egg	
F	Frog	
G	Grass	
H	Hat	
I	Ink	
J	Jam	
K	Kite	
L	Leaf	
M	Monkey	
N	Nose	
O	Oar	
P	Parrot	
Q	Queen	
R	Rope	
S	Sun	
T	Tap	
U	Umbrella	
V	Violin	
W	Well	
X	X-ray	
Y	Yacht	
Z	Zebra	

Now using the associated words as peg words, you can memorize a long list or even a speech! Let's see how to use the Alphabet Peg System to remember a formula.

Converting Celsius to Fahrenheit formula: **F=C×9/5+32**

Step 1—Convert

Hint: Use any of the Number Systems to convert the numbers.

F — Frog (Familiar Peg Word)
C — Cat (Familiar Peg Word)
9 — Wine (Number Rhyme System)
5 — Hive (Number Rhyme System)
32 — Man (Major System)

Step 2 — Story Link —A **frog** and a **cat** were drinking some **wine** from a **hive** made by a **man**!

Once you convert the story link back into the alphabets and numbers, you will remember how to convert from Celcius to Fahrenheit! In a similar way, you can use a combination of the Number Systems and the Alphabet Systems to remember anything alphanumeric such as passwords, passport numbers, Aadhaar Card numbers, etc.

Pro Tips:
- Since you already know 'apple' 'ball' 'cat' in order, you will automatically remember all the associated words in order.
- Don't spend too long creating these images. Just visualize them and immediately move on to the next item on the list.
- If there are more than twenty-six words to be remembered, make associations for the first twenty-six words till you reach Z, then start over from A and link a second object to the first image.

Chapter 5

Memory Techniques

PART FOUR: JOURNEYS, NICKNAMES AND MIND MAPS

The Journey Method

The Journey Method is also called the Method of Loci (locations), the Mind Palace, the Memory Palace and the Roman Room. It is a simple method of using landmarks along a familiar route such as the route from your home to your school or a route even within your own home, to remember information. You simply 'place' the information to be remembered on a familiar peg that you know well. Since it is a familiar peg, remembering it will automatically recall the associated information.

Location provides you with a coherent context that gives some meaning to the information that you are studying. It combines the Link Method and Peg Systems to associate new information to something that is well-known and familiar. It is a simple yet extremely powerful technique to remember long or large pieces of information and can be used to memorize long speeches, stories, formulae, poems, shopping lists, names of presidents or prime ministers in correct order, periodic table, key points to long answers, etc.

The Route Journey Method

The Route Journey Method takes you on a journey from one place to another, marking certain landmarks along the way. For example, picture the route that you take from your home to your school every day. Now, what is the first landmark that you see when you step outside your front door? It may be your front gate. Use your front door as the first landmark and the front gate as your second. After you leave your front gate, what do you see? A large tree? Great. Use that as your third landmark. Once you pass the tree, you may see a bakery. Use that as your fourth landmark…and so on, till you reach your final landmark—your classroom.

Once you have this route and its landmarks firmly fixed in your mind, you are ready to start using this technique to store further information that you may need to remember in sequence (or not). Simply associate the information that you want to remember to each landmark along the way from your home to your school. Here, the landmarks act as pegs since they will never change. All you have to do is hang whatever you need to remember on these pegs and go on a journey from your home to your school while remembering each piece of information at each landmark. Just by picturing the landmark, you should be able to remember its associated memory.

The following is the list of landmarks from your home to your school along with a list of what you need to do today. Using the Route Journey Method, let's try and remember everything that you need to do, in the correct sequence.

	Route	To-Do List
1.	Front door of house	Homework
2.	Front gate	Group study
3.	Tree	Basketball practice
4.	Bakery	Fill up petrol in bike
5.	Traffic light	Go to tailor for measurements
6.	Petrol bunk	Singing practice
7.	Lake	Chemistry tuition

8. Shopping mall — Pick up laundry
9. Front gate of school — Get watch repaired
10. Desk in classroom — Buy milk on the way home

Picture your route from home to school clearly in your mind, seeing all ten landmarks distinctly. Now associate each item to each landmark in the order that you would like to do them. Let's work out this exercise below.

Front door—Homework: Your front door is made of huge sheets of paper that you are writing your homework on.

Front gate—Group study: Your study group is sitting around the front gate, lobbing information back and forth over it.

Tree—Basketball practice: Imagine jumping high up over the tree to dunk your basketball!

Bakery—Fill up petrol in bike: Your bike is faint with thirst and so it coughs and sputters all the way to the bakery for some refreshing petrol.

Traffic light—Tailor for measurements: The traffic light is made up of measuring tape and red, orange and green buttons and pins.

Petrol bunk—Singing practice— _____

Lake—Chemistry tuition— _____

Shopping mall—Pick up laundry— _____

Front gate of school—Get watch repaired— _____

Your desk at school—Buy milk— _____

The Room Journey Method

The Room Journey Method is also called Memory Palace or Mind Palace. In this method, you simply use the objects in a particular room or many rooms as pegs for what you need to remember. Picture your living room. Scan the room from left to right. As soon as you enter, you have a shoe rack to your left. A little past the shoe rack is a sofa. Beyond the sofa is a bookshelf next to which is the TV set. Next to the TV is a shelf for DVDs and to your right is a settee. So, within your living room itself you have pegs such as:

1. Shoe rack
2. Sofa
3. Bookshelf
4. TV set
5. DVD shelf
6. Settee

Since the living room has only six items that you can use as pegs, you can journey to the next room if you want to remember a list that is more than six items long. The next room is your bedroom. As soon as you enter, to the left is the light switch. Next to that is your study table. Opposite you is your bed and next to that is your mirror. To your right, you have a cupboard. So, in your bedroom, you now have:

7. Light switch
8. Study table
9. Bed
10. Mirror
11. Cupboard

Now if you want to remember more than eleven words, move to the next room which is the kitchen and peg items there. As soon as you enter the kitchen, you have the sink to your immediate left. The microwave oven is placed further up. The stove is opposite you and to the right of the stove, you have the fridge. So, in the kitchen you have:

11. Sink
12. Microwave oven
13. Stove
14. Fridge

If you need to remember more than sixteen items, go to the next room and peg objects there. Once you can picture the layout of your home with all its objects in each room firmly in your mind, you are ready to start remembering lists, speeches, etc., by using these objects as pegs to hang your information on. Let's work out an example. Using the above room landmarks, try to remember the six physical divisions of India. Place each of these at the first six landmarks in the living room. Once this is done, start your associations.

1. The shoe rack — The Great Northern Wall of the North
2. Sofa — The Great Northern Plains
3. Bookshelf — The Great Peninsular Plateau
4. TV set — The Great Indian Desert
5. DVD shelf — The Coastal Plains
6. Settee — The Island Groups

1. Shoe Rack and the Great Northern Wall of the North: Picture entering your house. You're about to keep your shoes in the shoe rack when there is a shuddering earthquake, the whole house begins to shake and suddenly, there's a massive mountain wall growing below your feet taking you higher and higher till you can touch the clouds!
2. Sofa and the Great Northern Plains: You then get on your sofa and slide down the mountain into lush green plains.
3. Bookshelf and the Great Peninsular Plateau: You move on to your bookshelf but it has now become an upside-down triangle (the shape of a plateau)!
4. TV set and the Great Indian Desert— _____

5. DVD shelf and the Coastal Plains— _____
6. Settee and the Island Groups— _____

Now, if anybody asks you if you know the physical characteristics of India, simply walk through your living room picturing each characteristic on each landmark and you should be able to remember them all!

Pro Tips:
- Use familiar locations. Always move in the same direction (preferably left to right).
- Be thorough with your route.
- You can walk through your house and peg objects. However, it is better to use what you already remember since this is stored in your long-term memory.
- There is no limit to how many pegs you create and therefore this system can be used for remembering long lists, speeches, monologues, poems, etc.
- Landmarks such as door, gate etc., might seem like mundane objects, but make sure you enhance them in your mind, giving them some character or personality which makes them unforgettable.
- Make sure the journey follows a logical path. This will help you remember the correct sequence of items on your list.
- Using this method, you can remember the list in its correct sequence (by journeying from your front door to your desk), reverse sequence (journeying from your desk to your front door) or from any point (starting at the petrol bunk instead of your front door). In this way, you will be able to remember a speech forwards and backwards and even anywhere from the middle!
- Keep making your journey longer and longer to remember more information.

- Journeys can be made using any routes—routes from home to school, routes within a building such as your home, local supermarket, school, shopping mall, etc.
- To store information that you only need for a few hours (shopping lists, to-do lists), you can use the same room or route that you always use but replace or rewrite new information over old information. Once you have finished shopping, you can mentally remove these images from their landmarks, leaving the landmark empty and ready to use again.
- To store information for a longer period of time (periodic table, poems, speeches, formulae), reserve a specific journey for that piece of information only and make the journey appropriate to that subject matter. Review that journey and associated information from time to time so that you do not forget it but do not use the same route for any other information.

Nickname Method

How many of you have nicknames or special names for your friends or siblings? How many of you have naughty names for your teachers? Do you have a special name for your best friend? You may come up with nicknames for people based on their physical features, their existing names, some strange mannerisms that they may have or even based on their jobs! Sometimes, if you have two or more classmates with the same name, you might assign a nickname to them to distinguish one from the other.

Assigning nicknames to people helps you remember them better. You can apply the same technique of assigning nicknames to study material that you want to remember. Using this naming system, you can learn names of countries along with their capitals, currencies, etc. You can remember authors and their books, inventors and their inventions, and in fact, any kind of information that you want! Just remember to apply the basic rules of visualization, imagination, association and location to the information that you would like to remember as this will make it more concrete in your mind.

Let's look at the following countries and their currencies and see how we can break up their names to remember them better.

		Nickname	Association
Country Currency	Denmark Krone	Den + Mark Crone (old lady)	Old crone sitting in her den, putting a mark on her money.
Country Currency	Aruba Florin	Arrow bow Flowering	A bow shooting an arrow through a flowering plant.
Country Currency	Albania Lek	All + Ban Lake	All lakes are banned.
Country Currency	Armenia Dram	Ar + men Dam	Are men dammed?
Country Currency	Bangladesh Taka	Bangles + Desh Take	A country (desh) where you can take bangles

Pro Tips:
- Break up the word into smaller words or similar sounding words. For example, Germany can be broken up into two words i.e. Germ—many and Australia can be broken up into a similar *sounding* word i.e. Ostrich.
- Assign images to all words, whether they are abstract or concrete words. If the word is an abstract word such as 'honest', (hoe-nest) you can picture a concrete image like a garden hoe inside a nest. Do not picture another abstract word.
- Sometimes, instead of thinking of the word itself, you can think of something that you usually associate with that word. For example, if you are thinking of Egypt, you

can replace the word Egypt with an image of a pyramid.
- Make your associations personal. If you have actually visited a place that you are learning about, use the visual images that you experienced instead of thinking up new associated images. Since you have actually had experiences there, your memories would be that much stronger.
- Feel free to use your own regional languages to break up words. For example, Bangladesh can be broken into Bangles + Desh (country), Lal Bahadur Shastri can be directly translated to 'Red Brave' man.
- Use symbolic images when it is difficult to break up a word. For example, Switzerland is difficult to break up so you can use images that are generally associated with the country such as Swiss army knives, chocolates, watches, cheese, etc.
- This technique can help you remember a whole host of connected information. For example, the capital of Bulgaria is Sofia. It is bordered by Romania, Serbia, Macedonia, Greece, Turkey and the Black Sea. Picture a bull (Bulgaria) jumping on a sofa (Sofia) surrounded by a manic arrow (Ro-mania), a surfing bee (Ser-bia) with a big mac on its head (Mac-head-on-ya), Zeus (Greek god) and a turkey—all of them are trying their best not to fall into the Black Sea (Black sea and Turkey are self-describing images).

Mind Maps

This is an unconventional technique that helps you visualize and organise ideas so that you can understand your study material better. Most of the memory techniques that have been discussed so far only aid memory but do not help in understanding information. Mind mapping not only helps you understand what you learn but it also helps you see the information as a whole as well as its connection to other information. The technique of mind mapping is an effective combination of a memory aid and a thinking tool and therefore helps with understanding as well.

In everything that you study, whether you attend a lecture or study for an exam, you rely on your notes for information. Mind mapping is nothing but a more effective way of taking down notes so that you get all your information on one page. It helps you sketch out key ideas during a lecture and see quickly and clearly how each idea relates to each other. It also helps you put all your ideas and information together in one place in order to remember them better.

All this may sound complicated but it is one of the simplest methods to help you study. You simply need to map out your study material and write it down or draw it in a creative way. Information is noted, not word for word or sentence by sentence, but rather in the form of a diagram with lines branching out from one fact to another. Which would you remember better? A photograph or a thousand-word essay describing something? The photograph, of course! This is exactly what a mind map is—representing your study material in a more pictorial way.

Why you need mind maps:

- Mind maps help you concentrate on key points and provide a quick reference for revision before an exam.
- Mind maps can give you an overview of a large subject, at a glance.
- It encourages and strengthens associations.
- The combination of words and images with colours helps you remember the information better. Even if you use only colours to code your sub-branches and not images, you will be able to remember it better than your notes.
- It combines both left and right brain thinking, which means that you will remember it better than if it was just lines of words.

- Since it is your own interpretation of your study material, you will understand it better.
- It helps you map out your thoughts and assists you in brainstorming different ideas to work out a solution to a problem.
- Mind maps use all the functions of visualization, imagination, association and location thus enhancing your memory to its full potential.

How to make a mind map:

1. Start with a blank sheet of paper, preferably A4 or A3 in size and unruled. Turn it sideways (landscape).
2. Write down the main topic or the key word at the centre of the page. This can also be a diagram or image of the central topic that you are studying.
3. From the central figure or key word, draw branches radiating in different directions to signify sub-headings.
4. Add sub-branches radiating from these branches to show sub-headings of each branch. Again, these are drawn or labelled in different colours.
5. Be sure to make your branches curved and not straight lines. Curved lines encourage creative thinking.
6. Every time you add another word or image, draw a branch from the key words to connect with it. No matter how many branches you create, it should be possible to journey back along those branches to reach the centre.
7. Label the branches and sub-branches clearly and make sure that the images represent the subject matter clearly.
8. Branches or sub-branches may interconnect, depending on the strength of associations between them. Use arrows to connect linking ideas.
9. Make your map as colourful and beautiful as possible. You can use colours as themes as well, to differentiate one branch

or sub-branch from another. Colour helps with clarity. It also helps you recognize chunks of information by colour coding different bits of information and highlights important points.

Utilizing Memory Techniques

Every individual has his or her own unique way of learning, so try each of the memory techniques and discover which techniques suit you the best. For example, since you have the Number Rhyme System and the Number Shape System to translate numbers under 10 into images, you don't need to know both systems. Choose the system that you are most comfortable with and practice it.

You can mix and match the memory systems, as you will see in the following chapters. Again, choose the memory systems that you are most comfortable with and combine them. This will help you remember a combination of numbers and letters which will enable you to study historical dates, the periodic table, addresses, telephone numbers, etc. It is a matter of picking the techniques that you like and combining them in a way that fits your own thought process.

You can even make up your own systems using the principles of association, visualization, imagination and location that you have learnt in this book. Make it enjoyable and have fun. This way your brain will relax and you will learn new information quickly.

Chapter 6

Applying Memory Techniques in Academics

Now that you have learnt all the memory techniques, you will need to apply them in academics. Before proceeding, make sure that you are thorough with the memory techniques.

Learning a Second Language

Most people learn a second language or even a third language in school. The skills that you need to utilize while learning a new language include reading, writing, speaking, listening, understanding, memorizing and taking tests. Additional skills require learning gender-based words, grammatical rules, sentence structure, verb conjugations, prefixes, suffixes and basic roots of the language. For example, languages like Marathi, Bengali, Gujarati, Nepali, Punjabi and Hindi are all derived from the root language Sanskrit and, therefore, have similar words and sentence structures.

When you are just starting to learn a new language, memorization and repetition are the key. Since a new language is just a combination of sounds that initially hold no meaning, you need to give it some meaning so that you can understand it better. But simply translating from a second language to English may not be enough for this association to be strong. For example, the French word for dream is 'rêver' which does not sound like dream at all and has no memorable association to help you remember its meaning. However, if you give it a memorable association, you will be able to remember it better. Since the French word rêver sounds like the English word river, you can imagine a 'river of dreams' or 'dreaming about rivers'. This will help you remember both the French word and its meaning.

To learn a new language, you can use the Nickname Method. The key as always, is to use the memory building blocks of visualization, association, imagination and location to see the image clearly in your mind. Let's apply this system to a few words in French to help with vocabulary. Once you are done, read only the French words and see if you can remember their English meanings. If you need to remember the entire list of fifteen words, use the Pure Link System once you have finished learning the meanings.

	Meaning	Nickname	Association
French	Chou (shoo)	Shoe	A cabbage rotting in your shoe!
English	Cabbage	Cabbage	
French	Glace (glas)	Glass	Your window made of ice instead of glass.
English	Ice	Ice	
French	Fromage	From age	The old cheese is stinking from age.
English	Cheese	Cheese	
French	Craindre	Crane	I'm afraid of cranes!
English	To be afraid of	To be afraid of	
French	Bois (Bua)	Boa	The boa constrictor slithered up the wood.
English	Wood	Wood	

Pro Tips
- Always convert new words to more understandable words and associated images. See the image clearly in your mind. The more you practice, the clearer your images will become.
- By using visualization and imagination, create an association between the foreign word and its English

meaning and turn it into a mental image.
- You can either substitute other words or use a similar sounding word to create your mental image.
- Use the first image that comes to mind as this will form a stronger association.
- Understand the roots of the language that you are studying—everything from grammar to sentence structure. Try to expose yourself to the language as much as possible by watching movies, reading books, and trying to converse where possible.

Memorizing Historic Events and Dates

History is basically composed of a sequence of events, so you may need to remember the order of events to score better marks. To remember historical events along with their dates, you can use a combination of memory techniques. You can use the Number Shape or the Number Rhyme method or the Major System to remember the days of the month. You can use certain peg words for the month along with the Major System to remember the year. You can then use the Story Link Method to associate the date with the event.

The following are a list of twelve peg words to denote each month based on some event that happens in that month or an important day that falls in that month. You can either use these peg words or make up your own peg words depending on the month on which your birthday falls or what each month means to you.

Month	Important Event/Day	Peg Word
January	Wintertime	Snowflakes
February	Valentine's Day	Hearts/Flowers
March	Exams	Question papers
April	April Fool's Day	Joker

May	Labour Day	Labourers working in a field
June	Father's Day	Father
July	Monsoon season	Umbrella
August	Independence Day	Flag
September	Teacher's Day	Teacher
October	Halloween	Pumpkin
November	Thanksgiving Day	Turkey
December	Christmas Day	Christmas Tree

Always convert dates to the day/month/year format so that you do not get mixed up between the American System of dates and the British System of dates. So, if you want to remember that Jawaharlal Nehru was born on 14 November 1889, you first need to write it as 14/Nov/1889 and then convert the numbers to words using any of the systems. Here, you can use the Major System to convert the number 14 to **tire**, the month of November is converted to a **turkey** and 1889 is converted to its letters of **nffb**. Since 1 is common to most dates in the last 1000 years, you can disregard this and use only the letters for 889 which are **ffb**. The year is further converted into words using the Major System so you can convert 889 as **five** (88) **bee** (9) or **foe** (8) **vibe** (89) to denote the year 1889. Now you can use the Story Link Method to put all the words together including Jawaharlal Nehru.

Jawaharlal Nehru + tire + turkey + foe + vibe = **Jawaharlal Nehru tire**lessly used a **turkey** to fight his **foes**, which gave India a positive **vibe**.

Let's try this with a few more historically significant dates.
1. 29 March 1857—Revolt by Mangal Pandey at Barrackpore
   If you've seen the movie, you can clearly picture Aamir Khan as Mangal Pandey in his red uniform. The date '29' can be converted to either a duck and badminton racket

Applying Memory Techniques in Academics • 59

using the Number Shape Method or a **nib**, using the Major System. March is converted to question papers, 1857 can be converted to 857 or flk, which is then converted to a word—**fl**a**ck** or **fl**u**ke**. So you have Mangal Pandey + Nib + Question Papers + Flack. Using the Story Link Method, associate these words—**Mangal Pandey** furiously writing with his **nib** on his **question papers** and getting **flack** for it or **Mangal Pandey** hitting a **duck** with his **badminton racket**. It hits some British soldiers who are answering **question papers**, which is a **fluke**!

2. 1 September 1939—Second World War started.
   Using the Number Rhyme Method, 1 can be converted to bun, September is converted to teacher and 939 can be converted to bmp or **bump**. Second World War started when a teacher fired a bun with a bump!
3. 24 October 1945—United Nations Organization (UNO) was set up.
   Conversions—24—He**nr**y (Major System)
   October—Pumpkin
   945—brl—**Barrel**
   Story Link—UNO was started by Henry when he threw a pumpkin in a barrel!
4. 1905—Swadeshi Movement
   Conversion—905—pzl—puzzle
   Story Link—The Swadeshi movement was a **puzzle** to the Britishers.
5. 1942—Quit India Movement
   Conversion—942—brn—**Brain**
   Story Link—The Quit India Movement was started by using our brain!

Pro Tips:
- If all the events that you have studied are in the same century, then you can disregard the first two digits of

the year and concentrate on converting only the last two digits into a word or an image. For example, India's freedom struggle occurred between 1857 and 1947. If you remember the events that happened in the 1800s, you can disregard '18' and convert only the last two digits of the year.
- If you are memorizing events that happened in different centuries, you can colour code centuries so that you do not have to convert the first two numbers of the year. For example, events that happened in the 15th century can be assigned the colour red, events of the 16th century can be assigned blue, etc. Now when you visualize these events, just picture them with an overtone of the corresponding colour. This will save you the trouble of converting the 15 in 1598 into words or images.
- You can use any of the Number Systems to remember the dates, as long as you remember which system you used when converting the story links back to numbers.
- You can remember the entire list by using the Journey Method and placing each point or key word at one location.

Learning the Periodic Table

You have already studied the first twenty elements of the periodic table under the acrostic section. You can continue using acrostics for the entire periodic table by learning all the elements in their respective groups.

Group 1—The alkali metals—(H, Li, Na, K, Rb, Cs, Fr)
Highly Nasty Kids Rub Cats Fur
H—Hydrogen, **Li**—Lithium, **Na**—Sodium, **K**—Potassium, **Rb**—**Rub**idium, **Cs**—Caesium, **Fr**—Francium

Applying Memory Techniques in Academics • 61

Group 2—The alkaline earth metals—(Be, Mg, Ca, Sr, Ba, Ra)
Beer **Mug**s **Ca**n **S**e**r**ve **Ba**r **Ra**ts
Be—Beryllium, **Mg**—Magnesium, **Ca**—Calcium, **Sr**—Strontium, **Ba**—Barium, **Ra**—Radium

Group 13 —The boron family —(B, Al, Ga, In, Tl)
Bears **Al**ways **Ga**ve **In**dians **T**rouble.
B—Boron, **Al**—Aluminium, **Ga**—Gallium, **In**—Indium, **Tl**—Thallium

Group 14 —The carbon family—(C, Si, Ge, Sn, Pb)
Can **Si**lly **Ge**rms **Sn**atch Lead?
C—Carbon, **Si**—Silicon, **Ge**—Germanium, **Sn**— Tin, **Pb**—Lead

Group 15— Nitrogen Family—(N, P, As, Sb, Bi)
Never **P**ut **A**r**s**enic (in)**S**i**b**ling's **B**eer.
N—Nitrogen, **P**—Phosphorus, **As**—Arsenic, **Sb**— Antimony, **Bi**—Bismuth

Group 16— Oxygen Family —The Chalcogens—(O, S, Se, Te, Po)
Old **S**urf **Se**ems **T**erribly **Po**lluted.
O—Oxygen, **S**—Sulfur, **Se**—Selenium, **Te**—Tellurium, **Po**—Polonium

Group 17 — Fluorine family—The Halogens —(F, Cl, Br, I, At)
'**F**loor **Cl**eaner **Br**oken?' **I** **A**sked.
F—Fluorine, **Cl**—Chlorine, **Br**—Bromine, **I**—Iodine, **At**—Astatine

Group 18 — Helium family—Noble Gases —(He, Ne, Ar, Kr, Xe, Rn)
He **Ne**eds **O**U**R** **Cr**azy **Xe**rox **R**epairma**n**.
He—Helium, **Ne**—Neon, **Ar**—Argon, **Kr**—Krypton, **Xe**—Xenon,

Rn—Radon

First Row Transition Metals —(Sc, Ti, V, Cr, Mn, Fe, Co, Ni, Cu, Zn)
Scott **Ti**ckled **V**anna's **Cr**anium, **Mn**anager **Fe**d **Co**ld **Ni**uggets (to) **Cu**te **Z**ebras.
Sc—Scandium, **Ti**—Titanium, **V**—Vanadium, **Cr**— Chromium, **Mn**— Manganese, **Fe**— Iron, **Co**—Cobalt, **Ni**—Nickel, **Cu**—Copper, **Zn**—Zinc

Second Row Transition Metals—(Y, Zr, Nb, Mo, Tc, Ru, Rh, Pd, Ag, Cd)
Yes, **Z**ephyr **N**ob **M**ost **T**echnicians **Ru**b **R**od's **P**ale **S**ilver **C**adillac.
Y—Yttrium, **Zr**—Zirconium, **Nb**—Niobium, **Mo**—Molybdenum, **Tc**—Technetium, **Ru**—Ruthenium, **Rh**—Rhodium, **Pd**—Palladium, **Ag**— Silver, **Cd**—Cadmium

Third Row Transition Metals —(La, Hf, Ta, W, Re, Os, Ir, Pt, Au, Hg)
Larry **H**alf **Ta**med **W**endy **Re**sulting(in) **Os**sy **I**rrationally **P**leading (for) **Au**drey's **H**ug.
L—Lanthanum, **Hf**—Hafnium, **Ta**—Tantalum, **W**— Tungsten, **Re**—Rhenium, **Os**—Osmium, **Ir**—Iridium, **Pt**—Platinum, **Au**—Gold, **Hg**— Mercury.

Lanthanides —(Ce, Pr, Nd, Pm, Sm, Eu, Gd, Tb, Dy, Ho, Er, Tm, Yb, Lu)
Caesar **P**rocrastinated **N**eeding **P**ermission(from) **S**ome **Eu**ropeans (who were) **G**ood (in) **T**ubs **D**yed **Ho**ney, **Er**ring **T**hem(to) **Y**ell '**Lu**tetium!'
Ce—Cerium, **Pr**—Praseodymium, **Nd**—Neodymium, **Pm**—Promethium, **Sm**—Samarium, **Eu**—Europium, **Gd**—

Gadolinium, **Tb**—**Tb**erbium, **Dy**—**Dy**sprosium, **Ho**—**Ho**lmium, **Er**—**Er**bium, **Tm**—**T**hu**l**ium, **Yb**—**Y**tter**b**ium, **Lu**—**Lu**tetium.

Actinides —(Th, Pa, U, Np, Pu, Am, Cm, Bk, Cf, Es, Fm, Md, No, Lr)
Three **P**lanets: **U**ranus, **N**eptune, (and) **P**luto **A**im (to)**C**ome (to) **B**erkeley, **C**alifornia. **E**instein (and) **F**ermi **M**ade **No**ble **L**aws.
Th—**Th**orium, **Pa**—**P**rot**a**ctinium, **U**—**U**ranium, **Np**—**N**e**p**tunium, **Pu**—**P**l**u**tonium, **Am**—**Am**ericium, **Cm**—**C**uriu**m**, **Bk**—**B**er**k**elium, **Cf**—**C**ali**f**ornium, **Es**—**E**in**s**teinium, **Fm**—**F**er**m**ium, **Md**—**M**en**d**elevium, **No**—**No**bleium, **Lr**—**L**aw**r**encium.

Now that you have learnt all the elements in the periodic table, let's see how you can remember each group. Imagine a building that has thirteen rooms, one room for each group of elements discussed above. Maybe you can picture your school campus with its auditorium, library, labs, field, basketball court, etc. Now, let's take a guided tour around your school.

At the first stop, you have the school auditorium, where you will place the Group 1 elements. You can perhaps picture a candle burning at the auditorium door to signify the number 1 (Number Shape System) for Group 1.

Your next stop or landmark is your biology laboratory where you will place all the Group 2 elements. There is a duck (Number Shape for 2) standing guard at the door.

Continue in the same way for the rest of the groups.

The above exercise is important to visualize because the following exercise is connected to this and you will be revisiting these locations after completing the next exercise. So far, you have studied the list of elements in the periodic table according to their groups and you have placed each group in a particular location in your school. Next, you are going to learn the atomic number for each element. For this, you need to combine the

Nickname Method and the Major System of numbers.

Rather than go according to the atomic number of each element, you will continue to work with the above elements in their groups. Using the building blocks of visualization, imagination and association, picture each element with its atomic number in each location.

Start with **Group 1, which is in the auditorium of your school, with a candle at the front door.**

Element	Element Image	Atomic Number	Major System
Hydrogen (H)	Hydrogen balloon	1	Tie

Story Link—Hydrogen balloon dressed in formals, wearing a tie.

Lithium (Li)	Litchi	3	Ma

Story Link—Ma eating litchis.

Sodium (Na)	Soda	11	Tot

Story Link—Tiny tot drinking soda.

Potassium (K)	Pot stash	19	Tub

Story Link—Pot stashed in a tub.

Rubidium (Rb)	Rub	37	Mickey

Story Link—Mickey Mouse rubbing his injured knee.

Caesium (Cs)	Caesar	55	Lolly

Story Link—Julius Caesar is eating an ice lolly.

Francium (Fr)	France	87	Fish

Story Link—It's raining fish in France!

Story Link for Group 1:—Picture yourself entering your school auditorium that has a candle burning at the door. As soon as you enter, you see a hydrogen balloon, dressed up formally wearing a tie. As you go further in, you see your Ma eating litchis. Next to her is a tiny tot drinking soda, standing next to a pot stashed in a tub. As you move further inside, you see Mickey Mouse rubbing his injured knee while Julius Caesar is eating his ice lolly. Suddenly, it starts raining fish and you realize you're in France!

Group 2—Biology laboratory with a duck standing guard at the entrance.

Element	Element image	Atomic Number	Major System Image
Beryllium (Be)	Berry	4	Row

Story Link—Rows and rows of berries.

| Magnesium (Mg) | Magazines | 12 | Den |

Story Link—Aden piled high with magazines.

| Calcium (Ca) | Calcium Tablets | 20 | Nose |

Story Link—Shoving calcium tablets up your nose.

| Strontium (Sr) | Straw | 38 | Movie |

Story Link—A movie about straws.

| Barium (Ba) | Barry | 56 | Leash |

Story Link—Barry on a leash!

| Radium (Ra) | Radius | 88 | Five |

Story Link—The radius of that table is five!

Story Link for Group 2:—You leave the auditorium and move on to the Biology laboratory that has a duck standing guard at the entrance. As soon as you enter, you see rows and rows of berries. Once you have waded through all the berries, you come to a den piled high with magazines. Since the magazines are dusty and make you sneeze, you shove some calcium tablets up your nose and then decide to watch a movie about straws. In the movie, you see your friend Barry on a leash jumping up and down on a round table. He stares at you and says, 'The radius of this table is five, of course!'

Take a paper or a notebook and write down the rest of the groups in the same way as listed above. Once you are done, mentally walk through your school starting from the auditorium and moving through the biology laboratory, etc. and try to see these elements at these locations. While you are doing so, you can repeat the acrostic for each group in your mind so that you know the order of elements once you enter the appropriate location. Observing what these elements are doing (story link) will tell you their atomic numbers.

Pro Tips:
- While it has taken a few pages to describe this technique, remember that it takes only a few seconds to follow the instructions so do not despair about the length. Once you are proficient with the memory systems, following the steps mentioned above will be a piece of cake.
- Use acrostics to learn the elements in their groups. Assign each group to a different location in your school, using the Journey Method. Once this is done, use the Nickname method and Major Systems to link each element to their respective atomic numbers.
- Once you have finished the entire exercise from beginning to end, make sure you revise it so that it stays in your long-term memory.

Learning Poems, Monologues and Speeches

Ancient Romans and Greeks were good at memorizing and making long speeches. In fact, they took pride in their amazing memory to recall long texts. With little or no writing material available at the time, it was common for orators and poets to memorize their material by imagining a journey and placing each item that was to be remembered at a certain landmark. You can use the Journey Method as well, to memorize poems, monologues and speeches.

Poems

When memorizing poems, it helps to first read the poem and see how much you can remember without memory aids. Try to grasp the meaning of the poem, notice the syntax, rhyming words, and literary tools that the poet has used. For example, if it is a sonnet, you know that it will have fourteen lines in a particular rhythm. Study and read everything that you have been taught in class. This will give you a good context and a better understanding of the poem.

Let's look at the poem, 'The Road Not Taken' by Robert Frost. It has twenty lines and so you will have to plan a route that has twenty stops or landmarks. For this example, you can use an outdoor route from your front door to your classroom and fix twenty landmarks along the way. You can then peg each landmark to each line of the poem as follows:

'The Road Not Taken'
by Robert Frost

Front door of your house	Two roads diverged in a yellow wood,
Front gate	And sorry I could not travel both
Tree	And be one traveler, long I stood
Beauty Parlour	And looked down one as far as I

Traffic light	could To where it bent in the undergrowth;
Bakery	Then took the other, as just as fair,
Petrol bunk	And having perhaps the better claim,
Bus stop	Because it was grassy and wanted wear;
Restaurant	Though as for that the passing there
Bookstore	Had worn them really about the same,
Supermarket	And both that morning equally lay
Movie theatre	In leaves no step had trodden black.
Park	Oh, I kept the first for another day!
Lake	Yet knowing how way leads on to way,
Field	I doubted if I should ever come back.
Shopping mall	I shall be telling this with a sigh
Metro Station	Somewhere ages and ages hence:
Pub	Two roads diverged in a wood, and I—
School front gate	I took the one less traveled by,
Classroom	And that has made all the difference.

Step 1—Understand the context of the poem. Robert Frost was a farmer in America but he moved to England and was contemplating whether to take up writing or to continue farming. He was at a crossroad in his life and the decision that he was about to take would make all the difference.

Step 2—Write down the landmarks and the line to be pegged to each landmark side by side as above.

Step 3—Identify certain keywords in each line.

Step 4—At every landmark, make an association between the landmark and the first word of the poem in addition to the key word that you have chosen. In some lines, the key words may just be concepts and nothing concrete. In these instances, you will need to convert the concept into a more concrete word or image. For example, the line 'Though as for that the passing there' does not have a concrete image and therefore you will need to convert one of the words into a concrete image or word. The word 'passing' seems to be the keyword in that phrase. You can convert this into a concrete image by picturing Gandalf's famous line in *The Lord of the Rings* where he yells 'You shall not pass!' at the orcs. In the context of the poem, 'passing' refers to people who have walked that path before so you can also picture ancient Neanderthals trudging the same path as Robert Frost.

Step 5—If you cannot find a particular key word, use the essence of the phrase itself for an image.

Now go line by line, associating the location to the first word of each line along with the key words. Try and get the essence of the lines as well when you make your associations.

Front door of your house + two + yellow wood

Association—You can't believe it! All of a sudden, your house has two front doors and the wood has turned yellow!

Front gate + and + Image of man looking sad

Association—At the front gate, you see **And**y looking sadly at the crossroads.

Tree + And + One traveller
Association—**And**y has now moved to the tree and you see him standing there for a long time with his suitcase.

Beauty parlour + And + Looked

Association—Andy has lugged his suitcase all the way to the beauty parlour where he is peering intently down the road.

Traffic light + To + Bent bushes (undergrowth)
Association—At the traffic light, he can see a duck (number shape for to/two) under some bushes that are bent and crooked.

Bakery + Then + Took the other
Association—He picks up a hen (Then rhymes with ten, number rhyme for ten is hen) and walks in the other direction.

Petrol Bunk + and + Better Claim
Association—Once he reaches the petrol bunk, Andy butters a clam (sounds like better claim).

Bus stop + Because + Grassy
Association—At the bus stop, he sees a bee causing a traffic jam on the grass.

Continue on in a similar way for the rest of the poem.

Step 5—Now that you have completed the exercise, visualize your journey from your front door to your classroom with all twenty landmarks and see if you can remember the lines.

Memorizing Speeches and Monologues

The same method is followed to memorize speeches and monologues. First read through and study your speech or monologue and see how much you can remember. Then identify a key word in each line. Plan your journey and associate each key word to each landmark. When you are actually giving your speech, mentally walk from one landmark to the next, picturing each key word at each landmark and you will be able to remember your speech in the correct sequence.

Pro Tips:
- Always use familiar locations as the landmarks of these locations are already in your long-term memory.
- You may either use the Route Journey Method or Room Journey method for long poems and speeches.
- If the speech or monologue is very long, keep adding landmarks to your route. You can add as many landmarks as you like to associate each sentence or phrase of the speech or monologue.
- If you would like to remember your speech in paragraphs, use the Room Journey Method with one room corresponding with one paragraph. Objects in that room can be used as landmarks for every sentence or phrase.

Learning English Spellings
Words That Sound the Same But Are Spelt Differently (Homophones)

In most cases, you may know the spellings of words but may get confused about which word to use if two or more words sound the same but are spelt differently. For example, piece and peace, to and too, lose and loose, etc. In this case, if you learn simple memory techniques to learn one word, by the process of elimination, you would automatically know that the other word is spelt differently.

Three memory techniques can be utilized to remember the different spellings of these words. The first technique is the Nickname Method, the second technique is simple associations, and the third technique is using the words in context to understand the difference in meaning of the words. This is done by making sentences with the words, and using them in the right context.

Example for Nickname Method: Male and Mail—The m**al**e's middle name was **Al**.

Example for simple associations: Stationery and Stationary—If you associate the 'e' in stationery to 'envelope,' you will always remember that stationery refers to office materials while the word spelt with an 'a' refers to something that is not moving.

Example for context: Your and You're—**You are** (you're) intelligent, which means that **your** IQ is high.

Let's try these techniques with a few more words. Remember, by the process of elimination, once you know how to spell one word, you can remember the spelling for the other similar sounding word.

1. Principal and Principle —My school princi**pal** is my **pal**.
2. Quiet and Quite— Please keep **quite** qu**iet** about my d**iet**.
3. Meat and Meet —**Eat** some m**eat**.
4. Witch and Which —The w**itch** had an **itch**. **Which witch?** That **witch!**
5. Hear and Here —You h**ear** with your **ear**.

Pro Tips: When learning words that sound the same but are spelled differently, use simple memory techniques to learn one word. Then, by the process of elimination, you automatically know that the other similar sounding word is spelled differently.

Words That Are Spelled the Same But Pronounced Differently (Heteronyms)

There are a few words that are spelt the same but differ in meaning, pronunciation and derivation. Usually one pronunciation is a verb while the other is a noun. For example, she wound (verb) the bandage around the wound (noun). As with the previous section, use context to differentiate the meaning of one word from the other. It helps to understand the meaning of the words before you make sentences with them.

Given below are a list of words that are spelt the same (mostly) but have different pronunciations and meanings. Verbs, nouns and adjectives are denoted by V, N and Adj respectively.

Heteronym	Pronunciation	Meaning	Used in Context
Present	Prez-ent	N: Now	Since there was no time like the **present**, he thought he would **present** the **present** immediately.
Present	Priz-ent	V: Give someone	
Present	Prez-ent	N: Gift	
Bass	Bahs	N: Type of freshwater fish	A **bass** was painted on the **bass** drum.
Bass	Base	N: Lowest musical pitch	
Dove	Duv	N: Bird	When shot at, the **dove dove** into the bushes.
Dove	D-oh-v	V: Past tense of dive	
Object	Ob-ject	V: Express opposing view	I did not **object** to the **object**.
Object	Ob-ject	N: A thing	
Row	R-ow (ou)	N: Fight	There was a **row** amongst the **rows** of boatmen to teach how to **row** the boat.
Row	R-oh	N: Arranged in straight line	
Row	R-oh	V: Propel boat with oars	

Pro Tip: When learning words that are spelt similarly but have a different meaning, first learn the meanings of the words and then form a sentence, using them in the correct context.

Commonly Misspelled Words

There are certain words in common vocabulary that are confusing and are almost always spelled wrong. For example, is it definitely or definately? Is it disappear or dissapear? Professor or professer? The Nickname method and simple associations can be used to spell the correct word. Here are a few.

1. Separate or seperate? — There's **a rat** in sep**a**r**a**te!

2. Argument or arguement? **Argue** lost an **E** in an **argu**ment!
3. Embarrass or embarass?— It's really hard to emba**rr**ass **r**eally **r**ighteous and **s**erious **s**tudents.
4. Necessary or neccessary?— It is ne**cess**ary to remember the **cess** pool in the middle of the road.
5. Receive or recieve?— It's better to g**i**ve than to rece**i**ve.

Pro Tip: When learning difficult spellings, use the Nickname Method and simple associations to spell the correct word.

Effective Reading

Most of us study by reading our notes or studying from our textbooks. There are a few techniques to help you read your study material more effectively. Although slightly unconventional, these techniques will help you focus, concentrate and understand your study material better.

1. You can make your reading and learning more effective by speeding up your reading. Speeding up reading actually helps you concentrate better and in turn, helps you understand the material better.
2. The next step to effective reading is to tell yourself that you are going to read the material only once in order to absorb the contents. Avoid back-tracking and re-reading the sentences over and over again. This will help you focus completely on what you are studying. If you read your study material with the attitude that you will be reading it again anyway, you are telling your mind that it doesn't have to focus so much the first time since it will have a second or third chance at the same material. As you can see, this will prove to be a waste of time.
3. In case you find the material difficult to understand, make note of it but don't stop reading. You can always ask a friend

or refer to other sources of information for clarification later but continue reading at a steady pace. If you maintain steady eye movement over your notes, your comprehension will improve.
4. Use your finger as a guide to glide over words. While you are reading, your eyes stop for a fraction of a second at each word. The point at which your eyes stop is the point at which the information gets absorbed into your brain. Therefore, if your eye movement is smoother and you stop at the end of each sentence or even after each paragraph, you will absorb larger pieces of information and reduce the strain on your eyes. To do this, you need to use your finger to guide your eyes over words and sentences.

Pro Tips:
- Have a mindset to read your syllabus only once while studying.
- Use your finger to point to the words as you read them to speed up your reading and encoding process.

Effective Note-Taking

Notes are vital in your studies as they help consolidate long lessons and help you focus on the key points and what is taught verbally in class. This is where Mind Mapping comes into play. When you use mind maps, you get a clearer idea of the content along with its relationship with other sub topics within the main topic. As you hear the lecture, keep drawing mind maps, starting at the centre and branching out. Since you are going to be drawing relationships and writing single words for ideas and sub topics, you will not be wasting time writing everything down verbatim. You will be able to see the topic in its entirety on one page and will not be wasting your energy in writing non-stop over endless pages. Since you will be making use of both hemispheres of your brain, you will also be improving your analytic, logical, visual and imaginative skills, thereby increasing your brain power.

Pro Tip: Use Mind Maps to take down notes instead of writing them word for word or in shorthand.